BRUNHILDA AND THE RING

Jorge Luján

translated by
Hugh Hazelton

GROUNDWOOD BOOKS
HOUSE OF ANANSI PRESS
TORONTO   BERKELEY

pictures by
LINDA WOLFSGRUBER

For Patsy, celebrating her friendship,
talent and courage. – JL

To Antonia and Peter. – LW

Text copyright © 2010 by Jorge Luján
English translation copyright © 2010 by Hugh Hazelton
Illustrations copyright © 2010 by Linda Wolfsgruber
First published in English in Canada and the USA in 2010
by Groundwood Books

Groundwood Books / House of Anansi Press
110 Spadina Avenue, Suite 801, Toronto ON M5V 2K4
or c/o Publishers Group West
1700 Fourth Street, Berkeley, CA 94710

We acknowledge for their financial support of our publishing program the
Canada Council for the Arts, the Government of Canada through the Canada
Book Fund (CBF) and the Ontario Arts Council.

 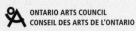

Library and Archives Canada Cataloguing in Publication
Luján, Jorge
    Brunhilda and the Ring / Jorge Luján; translated by Hugh Hazelton;
pictures by Linda Wolfsgruber.
ISBN 978-0-88899-924-5
    I. Hazelton, Hugh   II. Wolfsgruber, Linda   III. Title
PQ7798.22.U43B73 2010   863'.7   C2009-904752-7

The illustrations are prints combining drypoint and monoprint.
Design by Michael Solomon
Printed and bound in China

THE EPIC DRAMA of the Nibelungs, which Richard Wagner transformed into a transcendent opera, begins with the origin of life and ends with the destruction of the universal order. A multitude of opposing forces confront one another as the myth unfolds: the good and the perverse, lust and everlasting love, power and justice. Although there is no clear-cut victor in the struggle, avarice is punished and the kingdom of the oppressors destroyed. At the same time, however, unyielding law and ruses of darkness block the path of the heroes Siegmund, Sieglinde and Siegfried, who attempt to change the direction of events.

Out of the center of this maelstrom emerges Brunhilda, symbol of rebellion, love and compassion. In keeping with her ideals, she purifies the transgressions of the gods and heroes through fire and opens a breach of light leading to transformation. Her figure, at first divine and then human, always courageous and resolute, guided my vision as I wrote this version of the legendary and yet contemporary tale. Brunhilda's integrity, which makes her capable of challenging the law and renouncing her immortality for the sake of love, stands like an almost unattainable possibility for humanity — one that gives profound meaning to our presence on earth. — JL

Flow of water… reflections of time
remnants of dreams that people weave
carried away on the current.

I
THE GOLD OF THE RHINE

"RHINEGOLD! Rhinegold,"
sing Woglinde, Wellgunde and Flosshilde,
the happy Rhinemaidens,
as they splash about.
The innocent foam touches their breasts
and the deep riverbed
sleeps and shines with its treasure.

Suddenly a shadow appears
through a crack in the rocky depths.
A dark ray furrows the water:
Alberich, the Nibelung,
lunges toward the gold's guardians,
who dart away with horrified laughter.

"Valalaia, valay," they sing,
teasing him with shy caresses.
"Valalaia, valee!" they say,
snubbing him in their delicate way.
Without thinking of the risk,
Wellgunde recklessly reveals their secrets:

"Whoever forges a ring
from the gold of the Rhine
shall have the world at his feet.
Valalaia, valee!"

In graceful flight the Rhinemaidens brush against Alberich
as goosebumps cover his cold toad-like skin.
The dwarf pursues them, touching them as they swim,
but it's soon clear
that they're provoking and rebuffing him
without yielding a thing.

"To get the treasure,"
Woglinde warns,
"you must renounce love forever,
and who has ever known a creature
that could live without love's delight?"

"Ah! Then I'll curse love itself,"
cries Alberich and, swept up in his fury,
he breaks open a giant rock with his fist,
revealing the dazzling face of the gold.
"A curse upon love! I choose treasure instead!"

"Valaia, valee! Ah...! Ah...!"

The astonished guardians look on
as the dwarf grabs up the riches
and escapes back to the depths,
leaving the riverbed empty.

A dark peal of laughter travels over the waves
like a cruel, mocking echo of the maidens' lost joy.

Not far away, the giants Fafner and Fasolt have finished building a castle for the gods and are now demanding their pay.

A radiant castle on a rocky peak,
and at its feet, the Rhine Valley.
"Help!" cries Freya, goddess of youth,
as she flees the giants and runs downhill.
Fricka, goddess of marriage,
takes her in her arms and awakens her husband.
"Wotan! Get up! The titans
are on their way down
to make sure you keep your word."
Mountain crags crash around them
as Fafner and Fasolt stride forward.
"We've finished building Valhalla," they say,
"and we've come for Freya, our promised reward."
"What? That was only a joke,"
says Wotan, looking out at them from his one good eye.
"Aren't you the head of the gods?" replies Fafner.
"You won't get out of handing over Freya
and her golden apples,
the fruit that makes you gods immortal."
"Without those apples of theirs,"
Fasolt tells his brother,
"the gods will grow old and die."
Freya sobs, begging for help,
and Froh the rainbow-keeper arrives,
along with Donner, lord of thunder,
waving his hammer high, ready to strike.
"Stop!" cries Wotan. "We cannot kill them!
I engraved our pact in the runes on my spear.
If we break it, the world itself will end."

"Here comes Loge!" exclaims Fricka in relief.
"He promised to rescue Freya
and find some other way to pay the giants."
Everyone crowds around Loge, the god of fire,
but he brings unsettling news.
"I've looked everywhere," he says, "but nowhere in the world
is there anything that compares to the love of a woman,
nor is there anyone who would renounce it
except for Alberich, the greedy Nibelung,
who could not seduce the Rhinedaughters
and got even by stealing their treasure.
Now the maidens are begging you, Wotan,
to get their gold back for them and return it to the river."
"They're asking me, now, when my hands are tied?
I'm the one who needs help, not the one to give it."

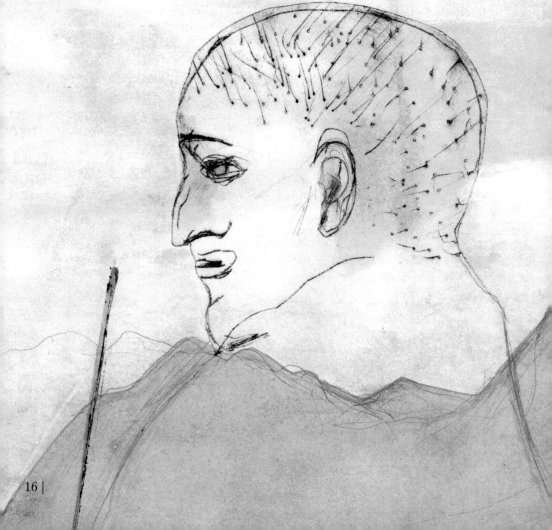

"A treasure?" asks Fasolt.
"And a ring," adds the fire god,
"that makes its wearer omnipotent."
"Let's go down and get it, Loge!" Wotan proposes.
"Good idea," says Fafner,
"but meanwhile, we'll settle for the gold!"
Loge insists it belongs to the Rhinemaidens,
so Fasolt throws Freya and her apples over his shoulder
and returns with his brother to the mountains.
"You'll have your pay by nightfall!"
Wotan calls after them, heartbroken,
as a dense mist surges up
and the gods begin to age.

Wotan and Loge head off for the underworld,
wrapped in drizzle and anxiety.

Wotan and Loge descend to the mines to recover Alberich's stolen treasure and trade it to the giants for Freya.

Scattered through the dark tunnels
the Nibelungs extract and refine their gold.
Amidst the din of hammering from the forge
one shadow is dragging another away.
"Let me go!" cries Mime the smith
to his brother Alberich.
"Your claws are going right through my neck!"

"First give back what doesn't belong to you,"
answers Alberich, shaking him from side to side,
and something falls to the floor.
"Aha! You thought you would hang on to the helmet, eh, Mime?
Listen to the spell, little brother,
and learn the magic of this thing you've created:
Misty night, nightly mist,
If you don't see me, something you've missed."
In a split second, Alberich disappears,
and an invisible whip starts lashing the backs
of Mime and the other Nibelungs.
"Go on! Get to work!" cries a voice
from everywhere and nowhere at once.
"Slow, steady labor and a just repose
are things of the past now. At last!
Get back to work for another's ambitions,
or just for misery itself.
Get working!"

Without being seen by the Rhinedaughters,
two silhouettes descend into the mines,
where they find not miners but slaves
clad in rags and moans.
"Hurry, Wotan," says Loge.
"Let's free these dwarves from their chains."
Mime sees them coming and
greets them with suspicion,
but ends up telling them of his woe.
"Once we Nibelungs lived happily
making necklaces for our wives,
but now we must plunge into our shafts
and tear out the gold that Alberich craves."

Thwack! The blow of a whip marks time. Whack!
Alberich emerges cracking his lash
as dwarves stagger by weighed down with ingots.
"Hey! What do you want down here?"
he asks when he sees the intruders.
"A kiss of the lash from the Master of Shadows?"
"We've come to admire all your marvels," says Loge.
"Ha, ha! You mean to covet what's shining!"
"Careful with your words, Nibelung.
Remember who gave you fire
to smelter the gold and create
    the ring."
"So what? I'm not afraid of you,
    fire-thug,"
replies Alberich as he spits on
    the ground.

"The dwarf's gone mad," says Wotan under his breath.
"Still," continues Loge, addressing the Nibelung,
"you have one major problem.
How will you keep thieves away when you sleep?"
"Loge, wise one, that's not so difficult,"
answers Alberich, showing him his helmet.
"When I put this on I become someone else.
So if you're plotting something, forget it right now!"
And, closing his eyes, he mutters,
"Monster, show them your fangs!"
The cave trembles and, where the dwarf stood,
a huge serpent springs forth with wide open jaws.
"We're astounded," Wotan remarks
when Alberich regains his form.

"But at times," adds Loge,
"great size isn't enough to save someone from danger,
since it only makes him more visible.
It must be harder still to shrink down like a toad
and scurry away between the cracks."
"Hard for you, fire-head,"
says Alberich, and adds,
"Being of the depths, wrinkle up without a doubt!"
The dwarf disappears, and in his place sits a toad,
and on the toad, Wotan's foot!
In a second Loge removes the dwarf's helmet,
and when Alberich reappears, Wotan ties him up.
"Nooooo!" His cry echoes down the tunnels.

Back among the peaks and fogs of Valhalla,
Wotan and Loge gaze at Alberich's prizes:
the treasure, the helmet and the ring.
"I admit I stole them," grumbles the Nibelung,
"but my act only affected myself.
Yours, though, will do in the lot of you."
"Do us in?" repeats Wotan scornfully.
"You won't be able to see us, we'll be up so high.
Get out of here, and slink back into darkness!"
"You're letting me go, are you?" says Alberich as he leaves.
"Then here's my thanks:
To get the ring, I had to reject all love,
but now that I've lost it, I'll curse it too!
Whoever sees this ring shall feel nothing but envy;
whoever possesses it shall live in constant anxiety;
whoever makes off with it shall have death by his side!
Use it, then, and enjoy my blessings!"

The treasure is recovered and Alberich puts a curse upon the ring.

Night is falling.
Out of the east come the giants with Freya,
from the west, Froh, Donner and Fricka.
"The wind smells of apples!" says Froh.
"A breeze that revives the gods," replies Donner.
The shadow of the titans spreads till it covers them all.
"Take the gold and let my sister go," begs Fricka.
The giants, loath to lose Freya,
sink their clubs into the earth before her.
"We'll only agree if you fill the space between these posts
so high with treasure that her beauty is hidden from view."
The gods speedily stack up the gold.
"I can still see her hair waving in the wind,"
says Fafner. "Cover it with this!"
Loge hesitates, but finally throws the helmet on top.
"I can still see one of her beautiful eyes
blinking through a crack," insists the giant.
Wotan evasively says he can't make out a thing.

"How about that shining ring on your finger?" says Fafner.
"Fit that into the crevice!"
Loge begs Wotan not to do it:
"Return it to the Rhinedaughters instead."
"If you do that," says Fasolt,
"then as you agreed before,
the goddess and the apples shall be ours!"

Suddenly, a blue light tinges the sunset.
Erda, the goddess of wisdom and the earth,
emerges from a cleft in the ground.

"Give up the ring, Wotan," she says,
"and escape the curse that awaits you."
Still the leader of the gods resists,
and Erda, calmly and sorrowfully, continues,
"I am the mother of the Norns,
the spinners of destiny. And I warn you,
if you disregard my advice
a black day shall come to Valhalla."
Erda sinks solemnly back into the ground,
and Wotan, seeing no way out,
throws the ring onto the pile of gold.
Fafner quickly gathers up the treasure in his sack
and then, seeing how angry his brother is, tells him,
"Calm down. The ring is yours if you want it."
But when Fasolt bends to pick it up,
his brother deals him a mortal blow with his club.
"Now dream away of Freya's eyes,"
grunts Fafner as he puts on the ring
and goes off to his dark destiny,
his back hunched beneath the gold.

To lift the gods' spirits, Donner shakes his mace.
Clouds clash: lightning bolts and rain.
Below them, the waters rise.
Slowly the sky begins to clear,
and a rainbow arches up to Valhalla.
"Let's cross now on the curved bridge," says Froh.

"Back to the castle," says Wotan, stepping forward.
One by one, the others follow him.
Loge brings up the rear, reflecting on Erda's words.

"Gold of the Rhine, return to us!"
the Rhinemaidens are heard praying below.
"Nobility and innocence have abandoned the river.
Wotan! Give us back our golden happiness!"

"Now that the shine has gone from your waters,"
Loge tells them dispiritedly,
"raise your eyes
and Valhalla will light up your days."

"Gold of the Rhine!
    Gold of the Rhine!"
answer Woglinde,
    Wellgunde and Flosshilde.
"We only trust what lies
    down deep.
The light of the gods is a
    fleeting mirage,
and their joy in the clouds
    is short-lived."

II

THE VALKYRIE

A WARRIOR, wounded and unarmed,
staggers toward a house
and pushes open an immense oaken door.
He goes inside and collapses on a bearskin
next to the fire in the hearth.
In the middle of the room
an ancient ash tree rises grandly,
extending its branches over the roof.
Stealthy footsteps:
A sad, beautiful woman
silently approaches the fallen fighter
and brings a cup of water to his parched lips.
"Who are you who offers such compassion
to a man as unfortunate as I," murmurs the warrior.
The woman shudders to hear a voice
that brings back memories of long ago.
"I'm Sieglinde, the wife of Hunding," she tells him.
Their eyes meet.
Refreshed by the drink, the stranger sits up
and gets ready to resume his journey.
"Who is pursuing you so tirelessly?" asks Sieglinde.
"If you rest here, at least tonight…"
"Misfortune is my companion," the wounded man tells her,
"and I must go now lest it also become yours."
A bitter smile crosses Sieglinde's face.
"There's no need to leave, then. Misfortune is no stranger to
    me, either.
You'll be at home here!"

*A reunion changes
the direction of
events.*

In the distance, the ringing of hooves sounds
    through the night.
"I am married," Sieglinde tells him,
"but not with my consent.
I was part of the booty pillaged by my husband's hordes."
The hoofbeats draw nearer and then fall silent.
A dark shape appears in the doorway.
"Who is this man?" the horseman wonders.
"He and my wife share the same serpent eyes."
With a measured voice, Sieglinde tells him
how she found the warrior lying defenseless in the room.
"If he expects to spend the night beneath my roof,"
Hunding warns,
"he'll have to tell his tale."

Siegmund tells his story.

The wounded man sighs
and begins to speak, as if to himself.
"I'm a son of the Wolf. That's what they call my father.
When the days were young,
a throng of soldiers murdered my mother
and kidnapped my beloved twin sister.
The men burned down our house while we were gone.
For years my father and I
wandered together through the forest
until the relentless trackers
forced us to take different paths to exile.
Nothing remains of our home
nor of our family…
Now the road is my companion,
and bad luck along with it."

"Anyone can see that the spinners of destiny
have not favored you," says Hunding defiantly.
"If the Norns haven't chosen you for their favorite son,
why should we humans do so?"

"Who are you fleeing from?" asks Sieglinde,
trembling with unease.
"Who is it we should protect you from?"
"This morning, down by the river," continues the stranger,
"I heard a voice asking for help.
It came from a young woman, almost a child,
who was to be married against her wishes.
Without hesitating I defended her,
but when the fight was over and the weapons destroyed,
I made my way across the field of battle
and found the girl among the fallen,
motionless, wrapped in rags,
her empty eyes
reflecting the flight of birds."

"And we've just spent hours chasing a wolf cub,"
interrupts Hunding.
"One who refuses to accept our beliefs and customs.
But after tracking him across hilltops and ravines,
I find my house has become his lair."

Sieglinde trembles as she thinks
of the woeful fate that awaits the warrior.
"I cannot refuse you shelter for the night,"
continues Hunding, "but when dawn breaks
you shall confront both me and death."
"With what weapons will this man defend himself
in the duel at daybreak?" wonders Sieglinde.
Hunding roughly grasps her arm
and drags her off to the bedroom,
but as she leaves
she casts an urgent glance at the ash tree.
A ray of moonlight breaks through its branches,
revealing the hilt of a sword buried in its trunk.
"Could that be the sword my father promised me?"
wonders the wounded warrior as he looks at the tree
and then sinks to the floor in exhaustion.

Later, a whisper of footsteps breaks the night silence.
"Are you feeling stronger, wanderer?" asks Sieglinde.
"Flee now, while my husband sleeps,
though before you go you must hear my story.
The day they forced this marriage on me,
Hunding and his minions had spent long hours
pouring alcohol down their gullets and shirt fronts,
when the door creaked open,
and there appeared a traveler with a gray cape
and a hat pulled low over one eye."
"I recognize that traveler," thinks her wounded guest.
"It's the daring old Wolf himself."
"Without hesitating, the old man
unsheathed a sword and drove it into that ash.
'This blade of steel,' he told us,
'belongs to the one who shall pull it from the tree,
for he will be the most worthy,
the most noble of all men.'
As soon as I heard that voice," says Sieglinde,
"I recognized my father
and felt a mysterious comfort."

"Sister!" exclaims the warrior.
"That sword in the tree is destined for me!
'Nothung,' I shall call it. 'Nothung!'"
He gets up, goes to the tree
and a second later
a magnificent weapon gleams in the air.
"Brother!" echoes Sieglinde.
"It is you, Siegmund!"
An embrace, long desired, seals their reunion,
and under the limpid moon
brother and sister
become lovers, too.

The terrible
command that
Wotan, under
pressure from his
wife, Fricka,
imposes on
Brunhilda, the
Valkyrie.

A radiant valley, with storm clouds in the distance.
On the edge of a cliff
two armed riders are talking:
Wotan, god of war, and his daughter Brunhilda,
with her blue eyes and long black hair,
mounted on Grane, her indomitable white steed.
"Valkyrie," says the god, "Erda the Wise and I
 brought you and your eight sisters into the world
so you could decide the outcome of battles
and carry the souls of the dead to Valhalla.
A supreme mission awaits you now.
Ride forth and bestow victory on Siegmund."
"Nothing would give me greater pleasure, Father,
but look down into the valley.
Your wife is hurrying this way."
Brunhilda can barely control Grane,
who kicks and jumps from one rock to another
and then runs off into a nearby wood.

"My wife again," thinks Wotan.
"Those old customs and worn-out habits…"
Surrounded by darkened mists
Fricka, the goddess of marriage, arrives
to insist that Hunding and Sieglinde's marriage cannot be broken.
"Would you then punish passion?" asks Wotan with indignation.
"What vow can remain firm
when those who pronounce it detest each other?"

"It's time to settle accounts, you libertine," Fricka warns.
Wotan is incensed, but does not have an answer.
"There's no way out for you," Fricka tells him.
"Your favorite Valkyrie will
make sure the marriage is honored,
and it will be you who gives the order!"

Brunhilda returns, galloping up the mountainside.
The landscape, moments ago so imposing and luminous,
is now a dark sea of clouds.
Wotan remains silent,
his single eye focused not
on his daughter
but on the harsh shapes of destiny.
His wife's dark words
still resound in his ears.
"If the Valkyrie refuses to defend the laws of marriage,
our purpose as gods
will be extinguished forever."
"What's happened, Father?" Brunhilda asks.
"I just met Fricka on the road,
and her smile made me shiver."
"Daughter, my steps have been guided by love for humanity
but my acts have not always been so selfless.
I no longer make my own decisions."
The Valkyrie can hardly recognize the Great Commander.
"Don't torment yourself," she tells him. "I am your will,
the one who carries out your every wish."

Wotan explains himself to Brunhilda. "Listen then to what I have never confessed," says the god.
"Long ago, when my youth was fading,
I conquered the world and relinquished love
to pursue power,
but I didn't find what I was searching for
and, filled with sorrow, longed for love once more."
Wotan tells her the story of the Rhinegold
and reveals that, through the magic helmet,
Fafner has changed himself into a dragon to watch over
    the ring.
"If Alberich were ever to get the jeweled circle back," he says,
"he would destroy us all, the Beings of Light.
I must recover what I gave him in payment,
but how can I do so without going back on my word?
Only a man, through his own free will,
could carry out what I am forbidden to do."
"Siegmund is that man!" cries the Valkyrie.
"Oh, Brunhilda," the god continues, "in cheating on Fricka
I've made countless women's bellies round,
engendering Siegmund and the line of the Volsungs.
After a surprise attack and fire
that cost us two terrible deaths,
I wandered through the forest with my son
and left him a sword as his sole protection.
But my wife is so outraged by my acts
that she demands I destroy the son I love.
The threat of the ring
forces me to betray him."

"Tell me what you expect from me," Brunhilda replies.
Annoyed, Wotan's sorrow turns to rage.
"Fulfill Fricka's desire, which is also my own.
Carry Siegmund off to die!"
The Valkyrie shudders.
"You who taught me to admire this young Volsung
are now asking me to snatch away his life?
Are rules more important to you
than all the wisdom of Nature?" Brunhilda asks defiantly.
"You didn't make me a warrior
to defend the wrong combatant."
"Obey me, or I'll wipe all the smiles
from the face I have loved so much!"
And without another word, Wotan heads down into the valley.
"Your fury against yourself," thinks Brunhilda,
"has made the weight of my weapons intolerable.
How can I grasp their hilt in submission
if I know I'll be destroying the son you love?"

Siegmund runs after Sieglinde through a gorge.
When he catches up to her, she begs him to flee on alone.
"Dishonored by a husband imposed on me
and blinded by this impetuous love,
I am not worthy of you, Siegmund."
"No one is purer or more valiant," her brother tells her.
"Hear how Hunding's hounds are closing in,"
she says, "and escape while there's still time, my love!"
Unable to bear her despair any longer,
Sieglinde loses herself in madness and memories.

"There's smoke, Father, and strange men.
Are you all still here in the wood?
Where is my twin, the other half of my being?
The house is burning, our enemies surround us,
and the smoke is blinding… blinding…"
Suddenly, an apparition fills the dawn.
Along the steep path comes Brunhilda
with Grane at her side.
She stops before them and tells Siegmund
he must accompany her to Valhalla,
where Wotan and the other gods await him.
An ancient joy revives the Volsung,
but when he hears he must leave Sieglinde behind,
his happiness disappears.
"Continue on your way, Brunhilda.
If my sister cannot come with me,
then nothing can make me follow you."
"It's not for you to question the decision, warrior.
No one can live on earth
once he has met a Valkyrie's fatal gaze."
"I fear nothing," says Siegmund.
"This sword, symbol of my father's love,
will grant me victory."
"Foolish man," replies Brunhilda, deeply moved.
"He who gave you that blade
is the one who has destined you to die."
Siegmund knows his end is near
and takes Sieglinde in his arms.
"My love," he murmurs. "He whom you trust
and for whose sake you have challenged the world
has been abandoned by his creator.
I shall no longer be able to protect you."

Brunhilda fearfully scans the horizon.

"Never will I leave my beloved
to join the frozen hearts of Valhalla," Siegmund tells her.

"The moment is nigh," Brunhilda warns.

"Entrust me now with your beloved and what you have given
her."

Siegmund resolutely raises his sword.

"If this weapon bequeathed me by a false benefactor
is incapable of striking down my enemies,
then let it serve to cut down these two lives."

"Stop!" cries Brunhilda. "Your courage has moved me
to change the outcome of the impending battle.

May triumph and happiness be yours!

Prepare now to fight.

Love's enemies are approaching."

Siegmund kisses his twin
and seats her upon a rock.
Soon a horde surrounds them.
Brandishing his sword,
Hunding leaps upon Siegmund,
just as Brunhilda protects him with her shield.
But when he prepares to strike back,
Wotan appears and breaks his blade with his spear.
Unimpeded now, Hunding laughs
and runs his weapon through Siegmund's chest.

The Volsung's death,
brought on by
Wotan, his father.

In the face of this inevitable undoing
Brunhilda gathers up the fragments of the sword,
takes Sieglinde in her arms and
gallops off on Grane.
Seeing death in his son's eyes,
Wotan lashes out in fury and fells Hunding.
"Will there now be peace with Fricka?" he wonders.
The offense against her ancient order has at last been set right.
Finding himself alone among the dead,
Wotan cries out, "Where is Brunhilda,
she who dared defy my commands?
She'll soon taste my punishment!"

"*Ho, ho, heia! Heia!*" cry the Valkyries
as they swiftly return from battle
with the bodies of the fallen
laid across the backs of their steeds.
They are ready now to ascend to Valhalla,
but one of them is missing.
There is a frantic galloping in the distance.
"Here comes Brunhilda!" exclaims Vaultrata,
"and she's bringing a woman!"
As soon as she dismounts, Brunhilda
tells her sisters she has defied their father
by trying to change the outcome of the struggle.
The angry reaction of the Valkyries
revives Sieglinde who, remembering what has happened,
begs them to kill her.

"No," Brunhilda tells her. "You can redeem your love.
Within your womb you carry a Volsung!"
Sieglinde trembles.
Her eyes shine like the dawn.
"Then save my child!"
Brunhilda advises her to flee into the wood,
where a dragon guards a golden treasure,
and hands her the shards of Siegmund's sword,
so that some day she may give them to her son.
"Your son," she says,
"will carry the name of Siegfried."
Sieglinde agrees
and runs toward the dark trees.

Wotan condemns Brunhilda to a defenseless sleep.

Roaring thunderclaps signal
    Wotan's arrival.
"Have you seen that damned
    girl?" he cries.
The Valkyries try to hide
    their sister,
but she steps forward valiantly.
It is fury rather than the god
    himself that speaks:
"You, who owe me everything,

shall be stripped of your chastity
and cast out from the divine family."
"You dishonor me, then, for having carried out
your most intimate wish?" cries Brunhilda.
"Silence!" shouts the god.
"I will plunge your rebellious spirit into a deep sleep,
and whoever awakens you will take your virtue."
"You would submit her to the caprices of a man?"
the Valkyries exclaim in alarm.
"You will wither us all."
"Do you dare defy me?" Wotan asks.
"Flee while you can
or share the fate of your miserable sister!"
Horrified, the warrior virgins
run off into the wood.
Lightning and thunderbolts
accompany their flight.
"You don't understand anything," says Brunhilda.
"When I saw the helplessness in Siegmund's eyes,
I was ashamed of your surrender
and decided to shield him."
"What do you know of helplessness!" answers Wotan.
"I had to tear a father's instincts from my heart,
though it meant the ruin of my world."

"If you still have a shred of pity,"
Brunhilda urges, "grant me one last desire.
Draw a line of fire around me
to frighten away those who would disturb my sleep,
so that only someone honorable might cross it."
"That's more than you deserve," answers Wotan.
"Then silence the daughter you once kissed so lovingly!"
    cries Brunhilda.
"Paralyze the one who made you happy as she grew!
But protect her with a bonfire
so that no servile wretch can touch her!"
"Dearest daughter," says Wotan, suddenly touched,
"light that opened a way for me through the storm,
lively companion that rode at my side,
if I lose you, I lose all I love.
May your nuptial veil be of fire, then,
and may the man who wins you
be freer and more just than I."
Wotan kisses Brunhilda on the eyelids
and, as she falls asleep, lays her down upon the moss.
Then he calls Loge to surround the rock with fire
and goes off, dejected, through the flames.

III
SIEGFRIED

"Miiiiimme! Miiiiiimmme!" calls a clear voice
from the entrance to the cave.
Mime looks out and finds young Siegfried
standing beside a menacing bear.
"Get rid of that beast, my son!" cries the dwarf.
"I'm not your son," answers Siegfried,
"and I'll only chase it away if you make me a sword."
"You'll just break it, as you always do."
"You call those needles you make swords?"
Siegfried laughs as the bear growls.
Frightened, the dwarf reminds him
that he's cared for him since he was a baby.
"That treacle of yours always made me sick," sneers Siegfried.
"Your cot gave me insomnia, your advice infuriated me."
"Perhaps it was because you were so ungrateful,"
Mime scolds, and takes a few steps inside
with the bear sniffing at his heels.
"No. It was because everything you do is wrapped in lies,"
the young man tells him.
"The wolf cub comes from the wolf, the lamb comes from the
    sheep.
What do I have of yours to make me believe that you're my
    father?
If you don't tell me the truth about my ancestry now,
I will have this bear devour you!"
A terrible roar blocks all hope of flight.
Cornered, the dwarf tells Siegfried of a woman
who died as she was giving birth to him,
leaving shards of metal called Nothung for her son.
"Then this very day you will make me a sword from them!"
demands Siegfried, and goes off with the bear.

*Siegfried urges
Mime, the Nibelung
who raised him, to
reveal his origins.*

The Traveler's visit
and the forging of
Nothung.

Mime is still complaining about the task ahead
when he hears footsteps outside.
A stranger with a hat hiding half his face
greets him and asks for shelter for the night.
The Nibelung is suspicious and refuses,
but the newcomer takes a seat and tells him,
"The road has taught me much.
Let's play a game.
I'll bet my head that I can answer
any urgent questions you might have."
Mime is dumbfounded
and asks things for which he already knows the answers.
"You've wasted your chance,"
says the Traveler. "Now it's my turn,
and if you make a mistake I'll have your head.
Who will forge Siegfried's sword? Who will be able to fuse the
　　fragments
that you stole from Sieglinde?"
When he realizes that he does not know the answer,
Mime smashes his hammer on the floor.
"You've lost your head," the Traveler tells him,
"but you can keep it for the moment."
And as he leaves he adds,
"The sword will be forged by one who knows no fear."

"I've seen too much," murmurs the dwarf,
"for my teeth not to chatter when faced with fear."
"What is fear?" asks Siegfried, who has just returned.
"The shivers," answers the Nibelung.
"The shakes…the frights…"
"Oh, I'd like to know how it feels!" exclaims the youth.
"I've heard of someone who could teach you about it,"
notes Mime with sudden enthusiasm.
"The dragon that guards the Cave of Envy."
"Ah! Then I must have the blade
that you're not capable of making," says Siegfried.
And he piles up coal
and lights the fire, which begins to crackle!
As he works the steel and hammers out the sword,
his clear song rings out through the wood:

"Nothung! Nothung!
Your laughing blue blade
will in thieving blood bathe.
Nothung! Nothung!
You saved not my father from death:
now defend his living son's breath."

"What a terrible paradox!" thinks Mime
as he watches Siegfried raise the sword.
"If this boy learns to fear,
he'll never be able to finish off the dragon.
And if he doesn't, he'll vanquish it,
and keep me from making off with the treasure!"

The hero confronts
the dragon Fafner
and finds that he
can understand the
language of birds.

Crimson dawn. Siegfried is watching
the dragon dozing outside its cave.
Suddenly, amidst the murmurs of the woods,
the song of a bird attracts his attention,
and he answers with his silver horn.
Fafner awakes, unbends his neck
and raises his head above the trees.
"Who dares approach?"
he roars, spying Siegfried.
"One who wishes to learn fear,"
answers the boy, sword in hand.
"That's a strange request
coming from such a puny mouthful,"
says the dragon and breathes out
a blast of fire that turns the dawn to noon.
"Hmm, with breath like that
the puny mouthful will move off like a shot,"
laughs Siegfried from a nearby crag.
"Foolish or daring, you'll meet the same end,"
growls Fafner, pulverizing the rock.
Furious, the dragon flails its tail,
demolishing everything around,
but Siegfried quickly leaps onto its foot
and plunges Nothung into its heart.
A gush of purple stains the air.

"Süeeggg…ffrriüeee…dddd," warbles the bird
from its perch in a birch tree,
"let the fluid cover your body,
and death will never touch you."
The boy is amazed to find
that his contact with the dragon's blood
enables him to understand the speech of birds.
Delighted, he begins to bathe in the dragon's warm liquids
when Mime arrives with a potion in his hand.
"Don't drink it," the bird warns.
"Your false father murdered your mother,
and wants to finish you off and grab all the gold."
Without a moment's hesitation, Siegfried raises the blade
and with a single blow cuts Mime's life short.

Hidden in the underbrush,
Alberich observes the scene
and smiles.

*Through the bird's
song, Siegfried
discovers his
destiny.*

A branch trembles and a leaf falls from a birch tree
onto the hero's back.
His entire body is covered in dragon's blood,
except for the spot where the leaf has landed.
Siegfried enters the cave to look over the treasure
but takes only two gleaming objects for himself.
Not knowing what to do with the rest,
the boy pushes in the remains of Fafner
and, to Alberich's despair,
seals the cave with them.

"Süeeggg…ffrrüieee…dddd," sings the bird,
"climb up to that peak amid the clouds
where Brunhilda, the Valkyrie, is sleeping.
She once refused to obey a despicable order,
so her father put a spell of sleep on her eyelids
and surrounded her with a ring of fire.
Rescue her and discover love!"

An unfamiliar feeling
quickens the young man's heart
as the bird traces a circle in the air
to guide him to the mountaintop.
Though unaware of their powers,
Siegfried takes with him
a helmet and a ring.

Wotan encounters
Erda, the goddess
of earth.

Not far from the dragon's cave,
The one-eyed Traveler comes upon Erda.
"Help me," he begs, "to overcome
this anxiety that torments me."
When she sees him, she steps back.
It is the same tyrant who years ago
took her by force, making her the mother of the Valkyries.
"Erda," Wotan confesses,
"our favorite daughter stood up to me
and I've condemned her to sleep
and awake as a mortal."
"What's this I hear?" says the goddess.
"The Great Rebel appeases those who rebel against him?"

"I understand your indignation,
but I must clear the way for a courageous young man
to rescue Brunhilda
and redeem the world through love."
"Take your footsteps far from mine, Wotan,
and let me return to the shadows.
Once more your wishes do not match your acts
and are sure to bring catastrophe."

Soon after, his face half covered,
the Traveler crosses Siegfried's path up the mountain.
"Don't take another step toward the summit," he warns.
"Look! The bird who was your guide has abandoned you,
because it saw two faithless ravens soaring
beyond the circle of fire."

"If that's all you can come up with,
get out of my way," answers Siegfried.
"Do as I say, or this spear shall break your sword
just as it did that of your father!" shouts Wotan.
"Was it you who killed my father?
A double lesson then my attack shall be!"
A powerful crack echoes like a thunderbolt,
and the Traveler's spear falls to pieces.
Quickly he runs away as a reddish glow
flickers on a nearby peak.
Siegfried eagerly climbs the mountain
and blows his horn to pass through the flames
that open as he steps forward.
There beneath the boughs of a fir tree
sleeps Brunhilda, not far from faithful Grane.
Siegfried approaches,
removes her helmet and breastplate
and surrenders to her beauty.
He kisses her
and she awakens with a shudder:
"Oh, Siegfried, sweet prize of my waiting,
you have returned the light to my eyes!"

"Brunhilda, everything around me is a mystery."

"Listen to what you wish to know, warrior.
I defended Siegmund, your father,
and have protected you since you first lay
within the womb of your mother, Sieglinde."

Lightning.
After a long silence
Siegfried pulls Brunhilda to him
and kisses her passionately again and again.
Tears flow down the Valkyrie's cheeks.
"Your sword opened the rings of my armor
and left me exposed and defenseless.
If I surrender to you, I will destroy all I have been.
The warrior revered by the strong,
she who was complete unto herself,
will be eclipsed.
Siegfried, I cannot find who I was!
Nor do I recognize who I am!"

"You were the dreaming virgin," says Siegfried.
"Now become my lover."
He caresses her,
and her clothes slip off
like waves drawing back from the beach.

"He who loves me, transforms me…
He who desires me, disturbs me…
In choosing love, I lose eternal life!"

"I will take care of you, I swear it!" says Siegfried,
as raindrops begin to fall from the sky.
"A strange mist is blurring my eyes.
I'm fainting!"
replies Brunhilda, as naked as the rain.

"Here only light surrounds you,"
declares Siegfried, kissing her all over.
"Be mine!"

"Though you do not know it, I have belonged to you forever.
But do not take what is precious from the one who loves you,
or destroy what makes you noble.
Like your image in a lake,
keep your lover pure."

"Valkyrie! Live for me now.
Let you and I be nothing more than love."

"Is love this thing that drives away my wisdom?
Is pleasure this feeling that devours me?" asks Brunhilda
as something takes fire in her breasts
and in her small dark garden.
"If so, let's laugh together
and lose our way…
Farewell immortality!
I am Siegfried!
You are Brunhilda!"

IV
THE TWILIGHT OF THE GODS

THE THREE Norns spin the threads of destiny
as they sing of Wotan the intrepid,
who bent down to drink from a spring
and gave one of his eyes
in exchange for love and wisdom.

They say the god saw the universal ash tree
and cut off a bough to make his spear,
but the wound began to dry up the wood,
then the forest, and finally the water that nurtured it.

They tell of the duel between spear and ring,
between Wotan and Alberich,
so different and yet the same,
each ready to use Siegfried
for his own ends.

They sing of Brunhilda,
the once immortal lover
cast out of the house of the gods
for having put love above the law,
and they wonder if she will be able
once again to decide the direction of the days.

We hear the song of the Norns, the seers and daughters of Erda.

Brunhilda awakes on a bed of sheepskins
and sees Siegfried standing with his back to her
at the mouth of the cave.
"Come," she tells him. "Don't stop being who you are.
What sense would it make to give up your dreams?"

"Valkyrie," answers the warrior,
"wherever I go, your voice shall guide me.
I will be faithful to you…"

"Go now. I will go with you
and you will always be with me."

"Take this ring," says Siegfried,
"as the sign and proof of our bond."

"And you, take along Grane, the one who flies over the fields.
He knows all of Brunhilda's feelings."

"Farewell, my moon and guide.
May the flames protect you till I return."

"Goodbye, sunchild,
love that fills and empties me.
In your absence I will learn to be human
and accept the face of death."

The two lovers say goodbye.

Beams of light enter through the windows
and sparkle like spears in the palace hall.
Three silhouettes are at the table: King Gunther,
Princess Gutrune and Hagen, the counselor.
"Tell me, Hagen, do you believe my acts are enough
to justify my stay on earth?" says the king.
A voice, bitter and metallic, answers:
"Now that you ask, King Gunther,
you still must marry some day,
as must your sister, the fair Gutrune."
"Who do you have in mind?" asks the king.
Hagen looks out the upper windows.
"I've heard of an incomparable woman.
Imprisoned by a spell, she sleeps on a crag
surrounded by walls of fire."
"How could I free her?" asks Gunther.
"Would valor be enough to break through the flames?"
"No," the counselor warns.
"That task is reserved for one who fears nothing.
Siegfried alone can rescue her for you!"
"The one who slew the dragon?" asks Gunther in amazement.
"Why would he do something like that?"
"For the love of the beautiful Gutrune, perhaps,
if she were to agree to win his heart."

"There's nothing I would like better,"
adds the princess. "But how and when?"
"With the rare tea of forgetfulness,"
        says Hagen.
"Whoever dares bring it to his lips
will feel an irresistible attraction to you
and all former love will flee his mind."

"You're as cunning as ever, brother," says Gutrune.
A heavy silence falls,
broken by the roar of a horn.
They run to the window. A boat is approaching,
and in it a warrior and a white horse.
"Hello up there in the palace! Where is Gunther,
King of the Gibichungs?
I am Siegfried, in search of adventure,
and I hope to fight him!"
With a small but firm gesture
Hagen signals the princess to leave.
"Siegfried?" calls Gunther.
"Every welcome awaits you here.
All that you see is yours!"
"You honor and amaze me with such a reception,"
answers Siegfried as he steps from the boat.
"I swear on my sword to be worthy of it."
"On your sword?" cuts in Hagen.
"But I have heard you possess gold and a ring."
"I'd almost forgotten about the treasure," replies
    Siegfried.
"All that I've brought from it is this helmet
                    that surely must be useful for something."
                    "That headpiece allows you to change
                        identity
                    or make yourself invisible," says Hagen.
                    "But where do you keep the ring?"
                    "I've given it to a sublime woman.
                    I'm sorry I can't share it with you."

The princess appears
at the top of the stairs with a goblet in her hand.
Slowly she descends
and stops in front of the visitor.
"Welcome to the land of the Gibichungs!
Let us toast to the fondness between us."
She hands Siegfried the goblet and he closes his eyes
as if to dispel Gutrune's splendor.
"I accept this drink and offer it to my beloved Brunhilda,
and the undying bond that unites us."
One swallow, however, is enough.
Brunhilda is forgotten. A single glance
leaves him in the blonde woman's thrall.
"Tell me, King," says the warrior,
"could the vision before me ever be my wife?"
"Nothing would make me happier," answers Gunther.
"It's a shame I can't also make the woman I love
my own. She's languishing
on a crag surrounded by flames."
"I'll help you conquer her love," says Siegfried,
as a cold shudder runs through his body
and then fades away like a dream.

*Siegfried learns
some things and
forgets others.*

Hagen brings in a horn brimming with wine
and asks Gunther and Siegfried
to shed a few drops of blood into it.
They do so, swearing to be comrades forever.
"Why don't you drink, counselor?"
asks Siegfried. "And add your vow to ours?"
"My blood isn't pure enough,
nor am I Gunther's full brother," says Hagen,
his eyes full of hate.
"We're the sons of the same mother,
but I was sired by the treacherous dwarf Alberich,
who won her over by using his magic helmet."
Once again a recollection struggles
to emerge from Siegfried's memory.
"I warn you both," Hagen continues,
"do not break your pledge or blood will flow,
and one of you will die to atone for it."
Gunther hurriedly changes the subject.
"Let's leave our scholar friend here with his troubles
and hoist our sails at once."
From one of the castle towers,
Gutrune and Hagen watch them sail off.
The evening sky is violet and heavy
with foreboding.

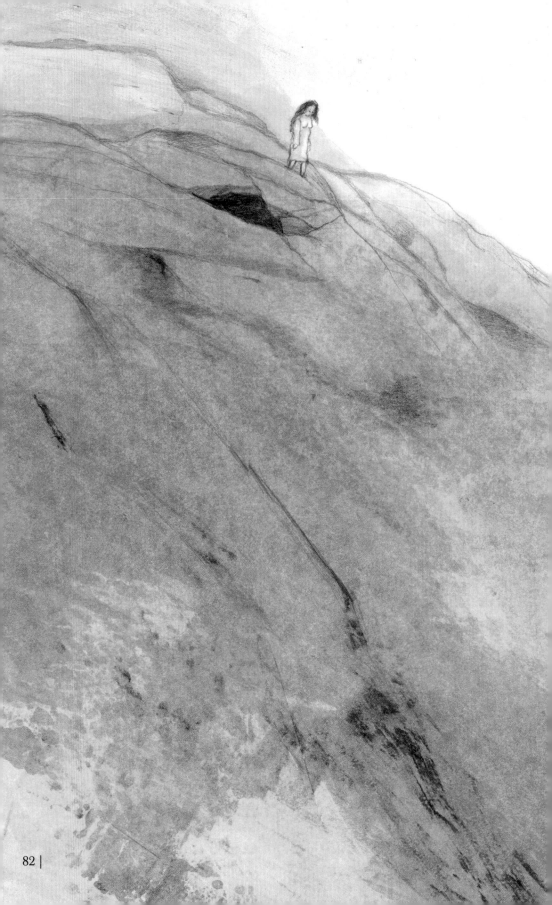

From her peak, Brunhilda scans the horizon.
A figure on horseback approaches over the lava hills.
"I've come to ask your help," says Vaultrata as she
    rides up.
"Wotan is piling up firewood all around the castle
and spurns the apples of youth.
He's waiting for the two ravens to return
before he makes his decision."
"He must want to put an end
to all his self-indulgence," thinks Brunhilda,
"and crush the free will
that led him to create Valkyries and Volsungs
to do battle in the world for the sake of love."

"Sister," says Vaultrata,
"that jeweled ring you wear is cursed.
Give it back to the Rhinemaidens!"
"How dare you say that?
It's the symbol of my union with Siegfried.
A single gleam is worth more to me
than all the flames that threaten Valhalla.
I no longer belong to that static world
and its rigid laws."
"Give up the ring, Brunhilda,
and put an end to the suffering of our creators."
"It is they who have made their own torments, Vaultrata.
Turn your horse round and ride back to them.
Don't cloud my passion with your whimpering."

Vaultrata's entreaty to her sister Brunhilda.

A sail crosses the sea's immensity.
The evening light brings the echo of a horn.
"My love!" cries Brunhilda. "Treasure of the world!"
A few moments later, Siegfried, unrecognizable,
    runs up,
leaping from one rock to another as the flames
    die down.
"I am the mighty Gunther," he declares,
wearing the helmet that renders his true self invisible,
"and I've come to make you my bride!"
"Impostor!" cries Brunhilda without recognizing him.
"Do not fear," replies Siegfried. "I am the King of the
    Gibichungs,
and in the dark of night you will lie with me."
"I'll never agree to such a shameful thing!
Through the force of this ring, I will vanquish you!"
"What ring?" says the counterfeit king, snatching it from
    her finger.
"Look!" he adds, "I'll even put my sword between us
as witness to the chastity of our encounter!"
"Who is this traitor?" grieves Brunhilda.
"Now I understand the long reach
of your punishment, harsh father.
You separated me from the lineage of the virgins
and exposed me to the pleasures of love,
only to deprive me of them afterward.
I tear you from my heart, Wotan!
I shall stand on my own feet
and forget you forever!"

Using the helmet of invisibility, Siegfried captures Brunhilda for the King of the Gibichungs.

While Hagen sleeps, Alberich whispers to him softly,
"Son, use your authority and vindicate me."
As he dreams, Hagen mumbles,
"I am your son only because you forced my mother.
I hate this life that forever denies me happiness."
"That denies it to us both," Alberich corrects him.
"But do you know what the Norns say,
those beautiful seers and daughters of Erda?
They tell that Wotan has been brought low by one of his
     children
who broke the spear where the pacts were written.
My curse has felled them all
except for that one guileless hero."

"Siegfried's help is only hastening his own ruin,"
thinks Hagen.
"Let us together destroy the arrogant gods,"
cries his father,
"and inherit their power!
Never will they understand that,
though we be creatures of the shadows,
we also long for the joyful light of gold
and the comforting radiance of the sun."

Standing atop Brunhilda's crag,
Siegfried takes a deep breath and, through the helmet's
    spell,
exhales, and is back with Gutrune,
asking her to be his wife.

The Valkryie meets the transfigured Siegfried, realizes that he has betrayed her, and is forced to marry Gunther.

"Behold your queen!" announces Gunther later
as their ship arrives at the castle's harbor.
"Siegfried, can it be you?" the Valkyrie asks in amazement
at finding her lover on the beach.
"Yes," he answers, hand-in-hand with Gutrune,
"and I'm about to be married."
Brunhilda trembles when she realizes he doesn't remember her.
"And how did you come by that?" she asks in amazement,
pointing to the ring and telling him that it was
Gunther who took it from her hand.
"I won it from a dragon," Siegfried answers,
and she, enraged, demands he tell the truth.
Adding to Gunther's embarrassment
Brunhilda declares, "But this man
lay beside me all night."
"I swear on your spear," Siegfried assures Gunther,
"that I never touched your bride!
And if I lie,
may I find death when it runs me through."
"So be it," cries the anguished Valkyrie.
"Besides betraying me, you've
now committed perjury."

Not wanting to hear any more,
Gutrune leads Siegfried off to the palace.
"I could help you avenge yourself," Hagen tells Brunhilda,
"if you have an idea how it might be done."
Beside herself with anger, the Valkyrie tells him about
the vulnerable spot on Siegfried's back.
The counselor immediately goes to the king
and speaks to him in secret.
"I'd never murder my blood brother!"
Gunther retorts. "What would I tell Gutrune?"
"Organize a hunting party," Hagen suggests,
"and we'll tell her he was killed by a wild boar."

Actors, flutes and smiles surge out of the palace
for the exuberant wedding party.
Brunhilda looks fiercely at Siegfried,
searching in vain for an answer,
but Gunther pulls her away
and makes her join the festivities.
The double wedding takes place
amidst the Gibichungs' revelry:
"May ten sons surround the king and Brunhilda!"
"May the sun smile upon the princess and Siegfried!"

A blare of horns announces the hunt.
In the river, the Rhinemaidens reminisce
about other, happier times.
Having lost his prey,
Siegfried wanders along the bank and watches them.
"What would you give us
if we showed you some bear tracks?" asks Woglinde.
"I don't know. I haven't even bagged a rabbit," he answers.
"How about that ring? Does that seem fair?" Flosshilde laughs.
"Oh, this thing?" says Siegfried.
"I took it off a snake with legs.
Should I trade it for some furry creature?"
"Yes, indeed!" Wellgunde tells him,
"or else the curse that hangs over it
will finish you off before day is done."
Siegfried, ever seeking danger,
is about to give in,
but Wellgunde's warning drives him away in disdain.

Siegfried disregards the Rhinemaidens' warnings and falls into Hagen's trap.

When he rejoins his companions,
he finds Gunther worried and sad.
To lift his spirits,
Siegfried tells him of Mime's deceptions
and the potion with which the dwarf
    tried to kill him.
"Speaking of potions," Hagen tells him,
"why not try some of this one?
It awakens memories that have
    been asleep."

Siegfried takes a long drink.
He begins to remember and tells
about the episode with the bird.
Carried along by his enthusiasm
and without connecting his experiences,
he remembers freeing the Valkyrie
and discovering love.
No one notices the two carrion birds
circling above his head.
No one but Hagen, that is, who rebukes him.
"So? You who know so much about the language of birds,
what is it those two ravens are cawing about?"
As soon as Siegfried lifts his gaze,
the counselor takes a step forward
and runs him through the back with his spear.
"Vengeance!" he cries. "Vengeance!"
The hunters retreat in horror
and then slowly form a circle around Siegfried,
who dies invoking a single name:
"Brunhilda!"

The two lovers are reunited once more in the arms of fire as we witness the downfall of the gods.

That night in the palace, Gutrune cannot sleep.
From one window she sees Brunhilda going down to the river,
and from the other a funeral procession
carrying back Siegfried's lifeless body.
The princess runs down, heartbroken.
"It was a wild boar! A wild boar!"
cries Hagen as he sees her coming
and loudly claims the ring as his.

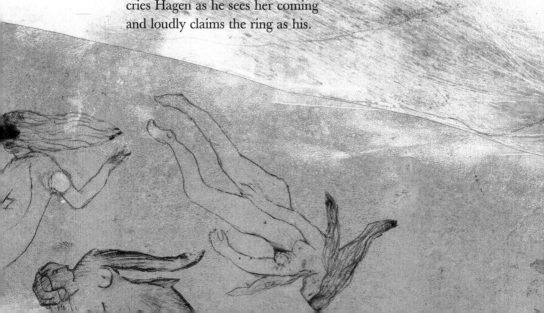

The king opposes him, whereupon Hagen cries,
"No one shall touch the ring of the Nibelungs!"
And, to the courtiers' horror,
he plunges his sword into Gunther's chest.
Brunhilda appears, pale and majestic.
Gutrune runs to her, sobbing,
and demands she avenge her husband's death.
"Dry your tears, you fraud!"
the Valkryie tells her.
"The Rhinemaidens have just told me
about the treacherous trap you laid.
Every step that Siegfried took
was always toward me,
until you joined the scheme
and offered him the goblet of forgetfulness!"

Then Brunhilda intones
a deep, sad funeral song
vindicating the hero's honor
and unmasking Wotan, the Great Instigator.

Hagen takes a step toward the fallen warrior
but Brunhilda stops him. "The ring's curse
can only be cleansed by the river."
And, removing it from Siegfried's still-warm hand,
she returns it to the turbulent waters.
The river rises and overflows its banks,
its daughters riding the crests of its waves.
In despair, Hagen leaps into the current.
"It's mine!" he bellows. "It's mine!"
But Woglinde and Wellgunde seize him
and drag him down into the depths,
as Flosshilde holds the ring high
in joyful triumph.

The Valkyrie orders
a funeral pyre to be set aflame
for the bravest and most noble of men
and, torch in hand,
gallops forth on Grane toward
    the citadel of the gods.

"Wotan!" she cries.
"You who condemn those who fulfill your desires!
Here's a burning torch for you!"
Throwing it onto the firewood, she shouts,
"Farewell to the gods and their inflexible wisdom!
May the law burn to ashes in the fire of love!"

As Valhalla and the gods are consumed,
the Valkyrie gallops back
and tears off her clothes
before Siegfried's funeral pyre.
With her hair streaming
and her cheeks and breasts burning
in the light of the leaping flames,
she urges Grane into the bonfire,
crying,
"Behold! Siegfried!
Your wife greets you with joy!"
And thus
does the brave Brunhilda
follow her beloved
through the doors of fire
and disappear from the face of the earth.

DRAMATIS PERSONÆ

Alberich: head of the Nibelungs, father of Hagen
Brunhilda: Valkyrie, daughter of Wotan and Erda
Donner: god of thunder
Erda: goddess of wisdom and the earth, mother of Brunhilda and the Norns
Fafner: giant, brother of Fasolt, dragon
Fasolt: giant, brother of Fafner
Flosshilde: Rhinemaiden
Freya: goddess of youth
Fricka: goddess of marriage, wife of Wotan
Froh: god and rainbow-keeper
Gibichungs: human tribe
Grane: Brunhilda's horse
Gunther: King of the Gibichungs, brother of Gutrune and half-brother of Hagen
Gutrune: Princess of the Gibichungs, sister of Gunther
Hagen: Alberich's son, counselor and half-brother of Gunther, King of the
    Gibichungs
Hunding: husband of Sieglinde
Loge: god of fire
Mime: Nibelung smith, brother of Alberich, guardian of Siegfried.
Nibelungs: dwarves who live underground
Norns: Fates, daughters of Erda
Nothung: magic sword
Siegfried: Volsung, son of Sieglinde and Siegmund
Sieglinde: Volsung, daughter of Wotan, sister of Siegmund, wife of Hunding,
    mother of Siegfried
Siegmund: Volsung, son of Wotan, brother of Sieglinde, father of Siegfried
Valkyries: Brunhilda and her seven sisters, the warrior virgins
Vaultrata: Valkyrie, sister of Brunhilda
Volsungs: human tribe
Wellgunde: Rhinemaiden
Woglinde: Rhinemaiden
Wotan: head of the gods, god of war, the Traveler, Fricka's husband, father of
    Siegmund, Sieglinde, Brunhilda and the Valkyries

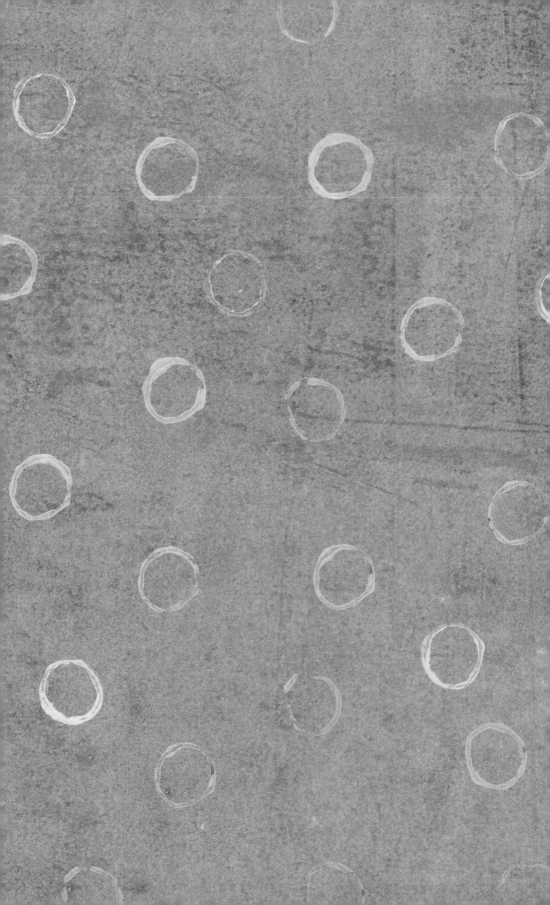